W9-AXE-892

This book belongs to
my friend:

_____

A NOTE TO PARENTS

In *The Brightest Star,* Dora and Boots journey to Star Mountain to catch the brightest star and bring it back to Dora's house for a party surprise. At each stop along the way, they use language skills and problem-solving skills to advance closer to their final destination. This story gives your child the chance to practice these same skills.

As Dora and Boots make their way to Star Mountain, they must identify the "highest hill," the "widest river," and the "straightest path" from among several possibilities. Before Dora and Boots reveal the correct hill, river, and path, ask your child what he thinks the right answers are. Talk with him about how he reached his conclusions. Explore this concept of comparisons (wide, wider, widest) with your child at home. For example, ask him to point out chairs or tables that demonstrate the different adjectives "high," "higher," and "highest." In addition, have some fun with this story by trying to guess the role that Luz, the brightest star, will play at the party.

Children love the night sky! After reading *The Brightest Star,* locate a simple star chart at a local library or on the Internet, and point out a few simple constellations to your child. If you can find a place away from bright lights, step outside and just look up! You can reinforce the skills learned in this story by asking your child to find the biggest, smallest, or even brightest star. You might also want to encourage your child's creativity by having him draw his own constellation or other image of the night sky.

Learning Fundamental:  problem solving

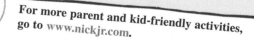

For more parent and kid-friendly activities, go to www.nickjr.com.

The Brightest Star

ENGLISH/SPANISH GLOSSARY and PRONUNCIATION GUIDE

English	Spanish	Pronunciation
Mommy	Mami	MAH-mee
Daddy	Papi	PAH-pee
Light	Luz	LOOZ

(In this story, the word Luz is used as the name of the brightest star.)

English	Spanish	Pronunciation
Hello	Hola	OH-lah
Good-bye	Adiós	Ah-dee-OHS
Thank you	Gracias	GRAH-see-ahs

Published by Scholastic Inc., 90 Old Sherman Turnpike, Danbury, CT 06816

ISBN 0-7172-6885-3

Printed in the U.S.A.

First Scholastic Printing, March 2004

The Brightest Star

by
Kitty Fross

illustrated by
A&J Studios

SCHOLASTIC INC.

New York   Toronto   London   Auckland   Sydney
Mexico City   New Delhi   Hong Kong   Buenos Aires

One sunny afternoon, Dora's *mami* and *papi* were getting ready for a big party.

Dora and Boots were making plans of their own. "Boots, I'm going to go catch Luz, the brightest star on Star Mountain," Dora told her best friend. "I need Luz for a big surprise for tonight. Will you help me?"

"Ooh! A surprise!" Boots said excitedly. "I love surprises. Sure, I'll help, Dora!"

"Great! Let's go catch the brightest star!" Dora cheered.

"How will we find her?" Boots wondered.

"Let's ask Map!" Dora said. "Map! Map!" she and Boots called together.

Map popped out of Backpack's pocket. "I know where
to find the brightest star!" he said confidently. "First
you have to go over the highest hill. Then you cross the
widest river. Then you follow the straightest path to the
top of Star Mountain. And that's where you'll find the
brightest star!"

"Highest hill, widest river, straightest path," Dora repeated. "Let's go, Boots!"

Soon Dora and Boots spotted three hills.
"That one's pretty high," Boots observed.
"That one's even higher," Dora said.
"That one is the highest of all!" they
agreed, and over they went.

"Now let's go catch the brightest star!" Dora sang out as they reached the other side.

Beyond the highest hill, three rivers stretched out.
Dora and Boots stopped in front of the first river.

"This river is pretty wide," Boots said.
"Yes, but we can use these stepping-stones
to cross over," Dora said confidently.
In a moment they were on the other side.

The second river was even wider
than the first.

"But we can use that bridge to
cross over!" Boots pointed out.

The third river was so wide that Dora and Boots could not see its far bank. "This must be the Widest River!" they agreed.

There were no stepping-stones. There was no bridge.

"How will we get across?" Boots wondered.

"Look, Boots! We can ride that raft across the Widest River!" Dora said excitedly.

Just then, they heard a rustling noise.

"Oh, no! Do you hear Swiper?" Dora asked. "He'll try to swipe the raft!"

"Swiper, no Swiping!" Dora and Boots said firmly.

"Oh mannn!" Swiper grumbled. Then he snapped his fingers and scurried away.

As they got ready to board the raft, Dora noticed a familiar figure in the distance.

"Boots, look! It's my cousin, Diego!" Dora said excitedly. "*¡Hola,* Diego!"

"*¡Hola,* Dora! *¡Hola,* Boots!" Diego called back. "Come see these giant river otters!"

By the riverbank, a group of huge otters was zipping and gliding through the water.

"Those are the biggest otters I've ever seen!" Boots said admiringly. "I wish we could swim like that. Then we would get across this river in no time!"

"Hey, good idea, Boots!" Diego said. "I'll bet one of these otters would give you a hand. I mean, a webbed foot!" he added with a laugh.

"*Mmmwip-ya-ya,*" Diego called.

The biggest of the giant otters swam up, yelping back at Diego. After a short conversation, the otter swam over to the raft and placed his front feet on it.

"Have a nice ride!" Diego told Dora and Boots.

Then, with a flick of his tail, the otter began pushing the raft swiftly across the river.

"*¡Adiós*, Diego!" Dora called out. "*¡Gracias!*"

"See you tonight at the celebration!" Boots added.

In no time, Dora and Boots spotted Star Mountain. They steered to the bank of the river, thanked the giant otter for his help, and walked to the base of the mountain.

"Map told us to take the straightest path," said Dora. "Do you see it?"

Up they climbed, following the straightest path.
All around them, they heard a chorus of high voices.
"Wheeeeeee!" the voices sang. "Catch me! Catch me!
Catch me!"

Soon they found themselves at the top of the mountain.

"Look at all these stars, Dora!" Boots gasped. "How are we going to find the brightest one?"

Three stars zoomed past Dora and Boots. "Catch me! I'm a bright star!" the first sang. "No, I'm brighter!" sang the second. "I'm the brightest star of all! Catch me!" called the third star.

"It's Luz! The brightest star!" Dora cried. "Quick, Boots! Let's catch her!"

Dora and Boots reached up high and clapped their hands together.

"You caught me!" the star sang happily.

Luz flew right into Dora's special star pocket.
"It's almost time for the celebration," Dora told
Boots. "Let's go home!"

Back at Dora's house, the celebration was getting started.

"Look, all our friends are here!" Boots said excitedly. "Is it time for the surprise now?"

"Yes, Boots! It's time!" Dora replied. Dora cleared her throat. "Everybody gather around," she called. "Boots and I have a surprise for you!" Then Dora reached into her star pocket. "Get ready, Luz," she whispered. "You know what to do."

Dora tossed Luz high into the air.
The shining star hovered there for a moment, then . . .
Hisssssss-BOOM! Suddenly the sky was alive with
bright, colorful fireworks.
"Wow!" Diego exclaimed. "This is a really good surprise!"

"It's even better than I'd imagined!" Dora agreed.
"Way to go, Luz!"

"I think it's the best surprise ever!" Boots said
happily as he watched the fireworks dancing
high overhead.